AMAZING OCEAN LIFE

Whales

by Colleen Sexton

Kaleidoscope
Minneapolis, MN

Where the Quest for Discovery Begins

This edition first published in 2023 by Kaleidoscope Publishing, Inc.

Kaleidoscope Publishing, Inc.
6012 Blue Circle Drive
Minnetonka, MN 55343

Library of Congress Control Number
2022937430

ISBN
978-1-64519-568-9 (library bound)
978-1-64519-638-9 (ebook)

Bigfoot Jr. lurks within one of the images in this book. It's up to you to find him!

Table of Contents

Ocean Giants

A whale bursts through the waves. It jumps into the air and lands. SPLASH!

Whales swim through water like fish. But they are **mammals**. They breathe air.

Where Do Whales Live?

Whales are the biggest animals on Earth. They are found in oceans all over the world.

FUN FACT
The blue whale is the biggest whale. It is even bigger than a dinosaur!

Many whales live alone. Some live in **pods**. A pod can have a few whales or hundreds.

Some pods travel to cold waters in summer and to warm waters in winter.

Whale Bodies

A whale has a rounded body with smooth skin. It slides through water.

Blubber under the skin keeps the whale warm in cold water.

The whale's tail ends in two **flukes**. The whale moves its tail up and down to swim forward.

Whales like to play. They jump, dive, and slap their tails on the water.

The whale moves its flippers to make turns.

The whale comes up for air. It breathes out a spray of misty water through its **blowhole**.

The whale breathes in fresh air. Then it closes a flap over the blowhole and dives again!

Parts of a Whale

Toothed Whales

Some whales have teeth to catch food. These whales dive deep to hunt for **prey**.

The whale makes a clicking sound. The sound hits a fish and makes an **echo**.

FUN FACT
Whales talk to each other with whistles, chirps, moans, and squeals.

What Do Toothed Whales Eat?

shrimp

crab

squid

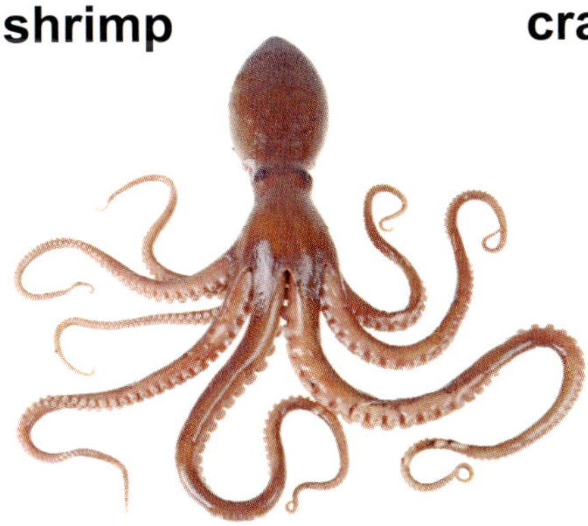

octopus

fish

The whale hears the echo. It tells the whale where the fish is. The whale chases the fish!

The whale grabs the fish with its teeth. It swallows the fish in one gulp.

Baleen Whales

What Do Baleen Whales Eat?

small fish

Some whales have **baleen** instead of teeth. These long plates hang in a whale's mouth.

A whale swims with its mouth open. It takes in a huge amount of **krill**.

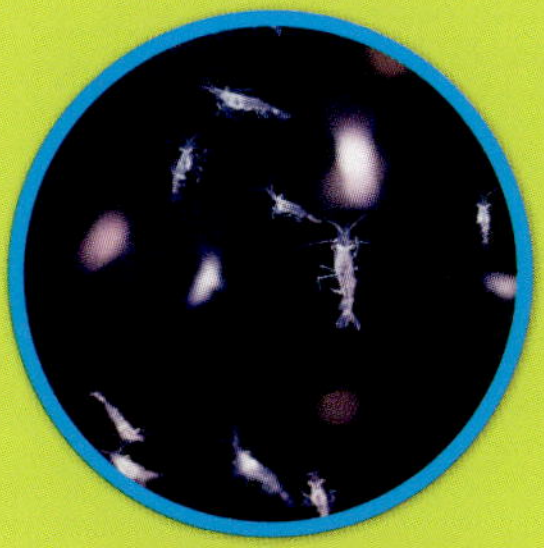

plankton

small squid

krill

The krill catches on the baleen. The whale closes its mouth and forces out the water.

The whale swallows the krill. Then it opens its mouth to scoop up its next meal!

Photo Glossary

baleen: Plates that hang down from a whale's upper jaws. Baleen skims food from the water.

blowhole: A breathing hole on top of an ocean mammal's head. Toothed whales have one blowhole, and baleen whales have two blowholes.

blubber: A layer of fat under a whale's skin. Blubber keeps a whale warm in cold water.

echo: A sound that repeats over and over after it bounces off an object. Whales make a clicking sound that echos when it hits a fish.

flukes: The two fins at the end of a whale's tail. Whales are recognized by their tail flukes.

krill: Tiny animals that look like shrimp. Baleen whales swim with their mouths open and eat a huge amount of krill.

mammal: A warm-blooded animal born alive, has a backbone, and drinks its mother's milk. Whales are mammals.

pod: A group of whales. A pod can have a few whales or hundreds.

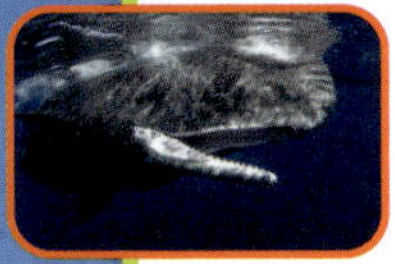

prey: An animal that another animal hunts and eats. Toothed whales dive deep to hunt for prey.

Read More

Gunasekara, Mignonne. *Wonderful Whales.* At the Aquarium. Minneapolis, MN: Bearport Publishing, 2021.

Leaf, Christina. *Whales.* Ocean Animals. Minneapolis, MN: Bellwether Media, 2021.

Ortega, Rena. *The Secret Life of Whales*. London: Thames & Hudson, 2021.

Websites

FACTSURFER

Factsurfer.com gives you a safe, fun way to find more information.

1. Go to www.factsurfer.com.
2. Enter "Whales" into the search box and click
3. Select your book cover to see a list of related websites.

About the Author

Colleen Sexton is a writer and editor. She is the author of more than one hundred nonfiction books for kids on topics ranging from astronauts to glaciers to elephants. She lives in Minnesota.

INDEX

PHOTO CREDITS

The images in this book are reproduced through Shutterstock: Maria Spb 3; Andres Avecedo 5; Ton Bangkeaw 6; Andrew Sutton 7, 22; Joost van Uffelen 8; Craig Lambert Photography 10, 17; Pascale Gueret 10; Tomas Kotouc 11; Marti Bug Catcher 12; Happy Whale 13; oksana.perkins 13, 22; Martin Prochazkacz 14, 22; bonchan 15; zhengzaishuru 15; koosen 15; Good luck images 15; SOMMAI 15; Earth theater 16; Krasowit 16; apiguide 18; kzww 18; M-Production 19; gowithstock 19; jo Crebbin 19, 22; I. Noyan Yilmaz 19, 22; Chase Dekker 20; John Tunney 21; optimarc 22; wildestanimal 22; Animalgraphy 22; OSTILL is Franck Camhi 22; Digital Storm 23. Cover: Sean Steininger, Willyam Bradberry, Solarisys.